Copyright © 1996 by Nord-Süd Verlag AG, Gossau Zürich, Switzerland.
First published in Switzerland under the title *Pauli komm wieder heim!*
English translation copyright © 1996 by North-South Books Inc.

First published in the United States, Canada, Great Britain, Australia, and New Zealand in
1996 by North-South Books, an imprint of Nord-Süd Verlag AG, Gossau Zürich, Switzerland.
First published in paperback in 1999.
Distributed in the United States by North-South Books Inc., New York.

Library of Congress Cataloging-in-Publication Data
Weninger, Brigitte.
[Pauli komm wieder heim! English]
Where have you gone, Davy? / Brigitte Weninger ; illustrated by Eve Tharlet ;
translated by Rosemary Lanning.
Summary: Falsely accused of breaking a pretty bowl, Davy the rabbit runs away
and finds the wide world to be a scary place.
[1. Rabbits—Fiction. 2. Runaways—Fiction.]
I. Tharlet, Eve, ill. II. Lanning, Rosemary. III. Title.
PZ7.W46916Wh 1996b
[E—]dc20 96-23317

A CIP catalogue record for this book is available from The British Library.
ISBN 1-55858-664-4 (trade binding) 10 9 8 7 6 5 4 3 2
ISBN 1-55858-665-2 (library binding) 10 9 8 7 6 5 4 3 2 1
ISBN 0-7358-1098-2 (paperback) 10 9 8 7 6 5 4 3 2 1
Printed in Belgium

For more information about our books, and the authors and artists
who create them, visit our web site: http://www.northsouth.com

# Where Have You Gone, Davy?

Brigitte Weninger
Illustrated by Eve Tharlet

Translated by
Rosemary Lanning

A MICHAEL NEUGEBAUER BOOK
NORTH-SOUTH BOOKS / NEW YORK / LONDON

Mother Rabbit had been out all morning looking for food, and now she was tired. "It's good to be home," she said with a sigh. But when she came into the burrow, she gasped. At her feet lay the broken pieces of a china bowl.

"Children, come here at once!" she shouted.

Dan came running.

"What's the matter, Mama?" he asked.

"Look at this mess!" said Mother. "Did you break the bowl?"

"No," said Dan. "You know I'd tell you if I had."

Then Donny and Daisy hopped in.

"Who did this?" Mother asked sternly, pointing at the broken
bowl.

"It wasn't me!" cried Daisy. Donny didn't say a word. He just
shook his head.

"Then who was it?" demanded Mother.

"It must have been Davy," Daisy said. "You know how careless
he is." Dan and Donny nodded.

When Father Rabbit came home, the children showed him the broken bowl. "Look what Davy did," they said.
"Oh, dear," sighed Father Rabbit. "Davy must learn to be more careful."

Outside, someone was whistling and singing. It was Davy.

"Listen, everyone!" he said as he rushed in. "I've just made up a new song!"

"No. *You* listen to *me*!" said Mother.

She held up a piece of the broken bowl. "How could you be so careless!" she scolded.

"But Mama . . ."

"You must have climbed on the shelf again. I've told you hundreds of times not to do that!"

"But Mama, I . . ."

"Out you go, out of my sight, before I really lose my temper!"

Davy trotted sadly outside.

He sat on the grass, put his head on his paws, and began to cry. "I didn't break the bowl," he sobbed. "Why wouldn't she listen?" He wiped away a tear. Then he stamped his foot. "It's not fair!" he protested. "I always get the blame! Now Mama even wants me to go away."

He sniffed. Then he stood up. "All right, I *will* go! I'll go out into the big, wide world! Then they'll be sorry, but it will be too late! I won't come back until I'm big and strong. That'll show them!"

Davy crept into the burrow through the
back door. He found his toy rabbit, a
small blanket, his bedtime book,
and the wooden boat his father
had carved for him.
He put them all in his pillowcase,
slung it over his shoulder like a
sack, and ran away.

Davy hopped across the fields until he came to a river. On the other side lay the big, wide world. How beautiful it looked!

Davy sat down to rest.
Soon it would be dark.
"I'll bet Mother and Father are looking
for me now," he thought. "But they won't find me!"
Feeling rather pleased with himself, Davy
leaped up—and got such a shock that
he ducked right down again.

A huge shadow swept soundlessly over him
and disappeared into the twilight.
Davy shivered with fear. He had forgotten
the owl came out at night.

Davy peered around anxiously. Then he picked up his sack and
ran—hippety-hop—until he was much nearer home.
He got out his toy bunny and his blanket, huddled down in the
grass, and waited. . . .

Someone was calling: "Davy, where are you?"
It was Dan.
Davy didn't move.
"Where have you gone, Davy?"
That was Mama. They were coming closer!
Davy shut his eyes tight.

"Darling Davy! There you are at last!" Mother took him in her arms.
Then she saw the pillowcase sack lying in the grass.
"Did you really want to run away?" she asked.
Davy nodded.
A fat tear rolled down his cheek, but Mama kissed it away.
Then she said, "Donny broke the bowl! After you went outside, he confessed. It was unfair of me to blame you. Will you forgive me, Davy?"

"Yes," said Davy. "I forgive you."
  They hugged each other again.
"Now will you carry me home?" he said. "I'm so-o-o tired."
"All right!" said Mama, smiling. "Up you go!"
  And she carried him all the way home.

"I found him!" called Mother Rabbit, and all the family came to welcome Davy home. All except for Donny, who stood in the corner, his ears drooping in shame.

Davy went over to his brother. "You're a very naughty boy, Donny!" he said. "But I'll forgive you if you promise never to do it again."

"I promise," said Donny, and they shook paws on it.

Then the rabbit family sat down to supper. Looking for Davy had made them all very hungry. And running away had made Davy hungry too.

Since one of their bowls was broken, Davy and Donny had to share. And they did it happily, now that all was forgiven.